RISING FORCE

CONNOR WHITELEY

No part of this book may be reproduced in any form or by any electronic or mechanical means. Including information storage, and retrieval systems, without written permission from the author except for the use of brief quotations in a book review.

This book is NOT legal, professional, medical, financial or any type of official advice.

Any questions about the book, rights licensing, or to contact the author, please email connorwhiteley@connorwhiteley.net

Copyright © 2024 CONNOR WHITELEY

All rights reserved.

DEDICATION
Thank you to all my readers without you I couldn't do what I love.

CHAPTER 1

Queen Augusta Windsoro used to love the absolutely wonderful Valley of Gold when she was a child, because it was just such a magical place. She loved running through the wide open fields, waving like a crazy child at the farmers that worked the fields and she was even told off a few times for stealing strawberries from the immense steep slopes that lined the valley.

She had spent so much wonderful time here with her mother and father and her brother before they all died. They would sing songs, take part in the duties and help the farmers and they would reward everyone in their kingdom of Octogi for their amazing work.

And even now Augusta loved her wonderful people. The people she loved, protected and would ultimately sacrifice herself for them.

But that valley from her childhood was most certainly dead.

Augusta stood in the middle of a wide open field

with immense steep slopes made from grey dirty rock rising above her, and the golden dots of her military had thankfully secured the top of the valley for her.

The valley was once filled with lust green grass, crops and joy, but now the ground was cracked, hard and charred.

The entire valley had been burnt, all the juicy delightful crops were destroyed and so many corpses laid around her.

Ever since Augusta had peacefully taken over the kingdom of Lordigo and Longmano through less peaceful means, she had changed her military to become a very effective fighting force but clearly it wasn't enough to save the brave men and women that laid dead like fish around her as she almost swam in a sea of the dead.

She knew that a detachment of her military was riding through the valley on their way to help strengthen the border with Jasper, the last free human land that was also the most powerful, brutal and evil of the human kingdoms. But that was clearly never going to happen.

She recognised a lot of the armour here. It was beautifully golden, well-crafted and bore her family's crest proudly on the breastplate but she also recognised the cold bronze armour of Jasper soldiers.

It was always one thing for Jasper to repeatedly sent her threats, assassins to kill her and threaten to burn her country to the ground, but invading this far into her kingdom. That was something else entirely.

"This is a mess," a very sexy male said.

Augusta grinned when her boyfriend Charleston stood next to her in his tight fitting and very beautiful silver knight armour. He was the best man she had ever known, he was so brave, delightful and clever.

And even though it had been a year since they had started dating ever since Longmano became part of her growing Empire, she still loved every single day and night with him.

The air smelt awful with hints of rotting flesh, smoke and charred flesh so much so that it overwhelmed her senses and Augusta coughed again and again.

She really hated Jasper.

"Jasper's gone too far this time and these attacks are only getting closer to home," Charleston said. "You do remember Owen's boyfriend was assassinated only last week,"

Augusta bit her lip. She truly loved Charleston's brother Owen, he was a King in his own right and it was just annoying as hell as gays could marry but they weren't allowed to be King. But she had made him de-facto King of Lordigo.

It was amazing and he had found love recently but Augusta still couldn't forgive herself for allowing the assassination to happen. Maybe if she gave him more guards, more protection, more of everything none of this ever would have happened.

"You know the kingdom will want answers and a plan," Charleston said.

Augusta hated it sometimes that he was always more regal and political than she was. All she cared about was protecting her people, the people she loved and her borders from invasion.

"You're right," Augusta said. "The generals and the two Lord Governors of Lordigo and Longmano will want a report on what I intend to do about Jasper,"

Augusta didn't really want to tell Charleston that she had read a spy report only yesterday that said that Jasper had two hundred thousand cavalry on their border and that wasn't including the one million soldiers and two thousand steam-tanks.

The invasion was going to happen very, very soon.

Augusta had tried to defuse the situation for ages by sending emissaries, ambassadors and even assassins but they all came back dead.

"What are you going to do?" Charleston asked.

Augusta just grinned at him. "I'm going to take Jasper before they take us,"

Charleston nodded and whistled and the military raced towards them to collect them.

Augusta knew there was a hell of a lot of planning to do and not a lot of time to do it in.

CHAPTER 2

Charleston was slightly more than relieved as him and sexy, stunning Augusta, wearing a very seductive blood red dress with golden threads and ocean blue highlights, sat down at a large brown oak coffee table. He was relieved that his stunning girlfriend wasn't too annoyed at him for already summoning his brother and the Lord Governor of Longmano, Lord Flinch, so they were already waiting for them back at the castle.

Thankfully she wasn't annoyed at all after she swore at him twice, maybe three times.

The wide perfectly polished grey stone chamber they were sitting in was beautiful with its immense stone blocks, roaring crackling fire behind them making it perfectly warm in the chamber despite it being the dead of winter and soon it would be spring, and the light fixtures were providing more than enough light.

Charleston had to admit that Owen looked great

in his tight white silk tunic that really did make him look regal and like a perfect de-facto king for their kingdom.

But Charleston really couldn't say the same about Lord Flinch. He was young but he looked so old because of his messy hair, unshaven beard and his clothes looked like he had been attacked by a wild cat or something.

Charleston forced himself to just focus on his brother as a very hot female servant bought them all large white crystal mugs of coffee. He really loved how thick, bitter and wonderfully refreshing the coffee was in Octogi. It was probably the one thing he didn't miss about Lordigo at all.

He took a sip and the sensationally warm liquid caused an explosion of flavour on his tongue. It was amazing.

But he still couldn't get the Jasper attack off his mind. He had been reading so many reports lately about Jasper attacks, from the invasion of a small town in the far south in Longmano that they had thankfully reclaimed, to the attack on a port on the eastern side of Lordigo and now the killing of so many troops.

This had to stop immediately and sadly Charleston knew that meant attacking and somehow claiming Jasper for themselves.

He knew it would be an impossible task because it was such a different culture, way of life and government system that he had no idea how the people would see Augusta.

So far everyone in Lordigo and Longmano saw Augusta as a saviour because she had saved them from his beast of a father and the madman that enslaved Longmano.

But Jasper was different. Its men and women were trained to be living weapons from birth, they didn't believe in democracy or a monarchy and they only believed in their Emperor.

Of course some reports had suggested there were millions of people that wanted their freedom from the Emperor but Charleston wasn't so sure.

The large wooden doors opened and a very tall woman wearing thick black metal armour walked in, and she sat down in-between Owen and Lord Flinch.

"Thank you General Cora for coming. I trust your engagements in Longmano were successful," Charleston said.

Augusta placed a gentle hand on his knee. "Actually the General here was hunting down the Jaspers that had attacked the valley detachment,"

Cora saluted the Queen and glared at Charleston. "The Jasper scum will no longer be a problem your highness. I would have hoped your boyfriend would have been more up-to-date. No offense your highness,"

Charleston didn't dare say anything. He knew exactly how popular Cora was in the military of all three kingdoms and she was completely dedicated to Augusta so that was enough for him to trust her, but definitely not like her.

"We need to take Jasper now," Augusta said.

Lord Flinch laughed and Charleston forced his own smile not to break out.

"Your Highness," Owen said, "I recommend we weaken them first,"

"Impossible," Cora said.

Augusta raised a hand. "That is exactly what I was thinking about. Jasper is far too powerful for us to take alone but, what if Jasper was weakened for us before we invaded?"

Charleston shrugged. "It's a good idea but I have no clue how you would do it. Sure, us stopping trade between our three kingdoms and Jasper had crippled them but they seem to be doing fine,"

"Because they're trading with the dwarves and elves," Augusta said.

Charleston nodded. That made a hell of a lot of sense but it was annoying because no one in the human lands really contacted and connected with the elves on their island empire that was easily three times larger than the human lands combined and the dwarves on their continent.

"We need support and need Jasper to be cut off and I believe we can help the elves at the same time," Augusta said. "Especially because intelligence reports suggest the Dwarf King and the Elven King and Queen are all fighting over a ring of islands three hundred kilometres off the coast of Longmano,"

No one said anything and Charleston really had

to admit that this seemed like a long shot at best. But Augusta was his queen and girlfriend so he had to support her because he loved her.

"There is a chance that the war will be over by the time we reach the ring of islands but if it means that Jasper is defeated then we have to try," Charleston said. "Me and the Queen will travel to these islands and the three of you should rule the Kingdom when we're gone,"

Everyone looked at Augusta.

She grinned. "Just defend it no matter what,"

Cora stood up, bowed and shouted how she would die before she allowed the kingdoms to fall. And as much as Charleston loved her commitment he seriously hoped that wouldn't happen.

Because he really didn't want his precious wonderful brother to be put in danger.

Cora, Lord Flinch and Owen pulled away and as soon as the large oak doors slammed shut Charleston just looked at the woman he loved.

"Think you'll have a kingdom to come back to?" he asked.

Augusta just laughed and he also wasn't sure if there would be.

CHAPTER 3

"It'll take us about three months to sail to the islands," Charleston said.

Augusta seriously couldn't believe what the hell she had gotten herself into. It wasn't that she didn't want to meet the Elven and Dwarf kings and Queen because they were meant to be great people, and if this plan worked then it would make her even more powerful. But the journey was a hell of a long one.

As Augusta leant against the cold damp wooden railing on top of her brand-new flagship, she stared out at the immense endless ocean with its perfect crystal clear blue water, small waves that gently hugged the ship as it sailed towards their destination and the delightful sun shone down upon them. so Augusta was really hoping it was going to warm up later.

The sound of hot sailors in short white shirts and sailor uniforms had certainly surprised her and Charleston but that only showed how little experience she had travelling by ship. It just wasn't really the done thing.

The entire flagship she had to admit was a stunner, an absolute stunner with it being the tallest and longest warship in human lands, the thick cream-coloured wood could withstand impacts of cannons, magic fire and even the most aggressive sea monsters. Well, at least that's what the seller had said to her.

The entire ship was a sheer marvel of human engineering and she was really looking forward to getting involved in a naval battle with Jasper because right now, Jasper was the ruler of the seas.

She had been reading plenty of reports recently about how Jasper was burning all dwarf ships that had entered or not entered its waters by mistake.

The amazing smell of sea, sweat and Charleston's wonderful manly musk filled her senses and she had plenty of carry pigeons to use for her royal duties so she could be productive in the next three months.

Thankfully her dragon Cargo, who had been really busying spying and freeing set his dragon friends in Jasper for months had promised to return.

If he had returned earlier they could simply fly to the ring of islands within a few days but Cargo didn't like flying in tens of hours at a time apparently. It was a shame.

Charleston came behind her and kissed her. Augusta smiled and turned around and pulled him closer. She really did love him, he was utterly amazing.

"What's your plan for making sure the dwarfs don't think we're Jasper?" Charleston asked.

Augusta pointed to the immense main sails that were starting to drop in massive waves that had immense symbols of her crest and dwarf and elven words saying that they were friendly. She didn't know if the words would be believed but she really, really hoped they wouldn't be attacked before the mission had even started.

"So what do you know about this ring of islands?" Charleston asked.

Augusta shrugged. "I could only send one emissary to the dwarfs because of how much they hate humans right now. She couldn't tell me a lot because the dwarfs would always tell her reports but she did tell me once that the ring of islands is called The Ring Of Magic in the dwarf language,"

Charleston nodded and Augusta focused on a massive seagull that flew around the ship a few times before going away again.

"She believed the dwarfs want the island because it contains magic they want, and two of the islands are built out entirely of stone so the dwarfs could mine them for thousands of years,"

"That explains the elves too," Charleston said. "And I take it the Ring of Magic is closer to their territory too,"

"Yes. The Elves call the Ring always hell though, they call it the Halo Of Death and no one understands why. I've spoken to some merchants that trade with the elves and they told me to stay away from this matter,"

Charleston shook his head and she knew why. Even she couldn't understand why merchants would risk offending her so that only made their words even more important. Something had to be happening on that ring of islands that each of the species didn't want the other doing.

"So we have to break peace between two species that hate each other, convince them to trade supplying and trading with Jasper and we then have to return to our kingdoms before Jasper invades and kill all our people,"

Augusta laughed. Charleston was so right and as much as she didn't want him to be so, she just couldn't ignore the tight knotting of her stomach as she realised that was exactly what was at stake.

The loud flapping of wings made Augusta look behind them and she waved as her beautiful dragon Cargo with his large blue scales and wonderful dragon body flew towards them.

He stopped just behind the ship and the mark linking her and Cargo mentally and physically together, a dagger burn mark into her hand, glowed and she knew he was going to help them.

Cargo flapped his wings slowly and then started to speed them up and the ship moved faster and faster.

"Thank you," Augusta said.

With the flagship racing through the wonderfully

calm water, the sun starting to heat up the air and an impossible mission in the distance, Augusta was really looking forward to this trip a lot more than she ever wanted to admit.

CHAPTER 4

Over the next month and a half, Charleston was seriously impressed with how strong, determined and powerful Cargo actually was. They had managed to half their travel time and even that had felt painfully long with there only being so many things he could do on the flagship.

Whilst Augusta had been busy with matters of state, empire and defence, he had forced himself to become a crew member, run around the ship twice a day and make sure that Augusta was prepared for her meeting with the elves and dwarfs.

Something that they had actually agreed to do because Augusta had been amazing enough to send a carrier pigeon to the ring of islands.

Charleston still wasn't sure if he liked the idea of this trip but he was only on here to protect the love of his life and that would just sadly have to do.

On the 45th morning, Charleston leant against the icy cold wooden railing at the stern of the ship and he smiled as the sun rose in front of them and he got the very first sight of their target destination, and it was seriously a lot more stunning than he ever could have imagined.

After only seeing seagulls, whales and sea monsters for so long, it was so great to see fresh dry land in the distance. Charleston had wanted to see an island for so long but he had only seen dark blue ocean after ocean after ocean.

The islands were hard to make out because of the intense orange of the sunlight but the islands were immense. They seemed to stretch out across the entire horizon and it seemed just impossible for one species to conquer all of this.

It surely would have made a lot more sense to simply divide up the islands between themselves instead of fighting over them. And the immensely thick columns of black smoke rising to veil parts of the rising sun hardly convinced them they were going to get peace at all here.

Charleston so badly wanted this mission to go well, because he had somehow managed to only fall in love more and more with Augusta over the past 45 days. She was so calm, clever and she was so determined to protect her people that Charleston was deadly sure that she didn't have a single flaw.

And she wouldn't say anything different about him.

The smell of the salty sea, sweat and musk from the crew started to disappear as the islands got closer, and Charleston was surprised at the delightful hints of mint, jasmine and freshly brewed tea that filled his senses.

"Get back inside your highness. It ain't safe," a woman said.

"I command you to let me go,"

Charleston popped his head over the other wooden railing that prevented whoever was steering the ship from falling onto the main deck of the ship.

Charleston watched as the first mate of the ship held the door to Augusta's and his cabin shut with Augusta pounding on the door.

"Report," Charleston said.

The woman jumped and Augusta slammed the door open so hard it smashed into the woman's nose.

"Commander Charleston," the woman said bowing slightly. "The black smoke in the distance is a threat to the Queen. If the enemy attack, I cannot risk the Queen getting hit,"

Charleston slowly nodded. "Thank you for your concern first-mate. Please return to your duties. I will return the Queen to her cabin if we are attacked, I promise you that,"

Augusta gave him a sideways look and he didn't care that she wasn't impressed with him. He didn't want the first-mate not to care about the queen in case there was a time she was in danger but he wasn't around to protect her.

Augusta came up the wooden stairs to see him. He wondered if she was going to moan at him but she kissed him and focused on the islands on the horizon.

"Beautiful, aren't they?" Augusta asked.

"Not as beautiful as you, but they come a close second," Charleston said.

"I assume the elves know we're here and they will be sending their ships to escort us or something,"

"We will be okay. The cannons are always loaded, the men and women are always prepared for battle and it isn't like the elves were happy to get your message,"

Augusta nodded, but it wasn't that energetic so he knew she was only nodding to be kind.

"We will be protected and I really hope we aren't attacked," Augusta said.

Charleston wasn't a fan of Augusta wasn't sure about what was going to happen next. This would be the first high-level talk between the monarchs of dwarfs, elves and humans in so long that Charleston didn't dare let this go wrong.

But as the air grew colder and he couldn't shake the feeling that he was being watched, he just knew that something was coming for them.

And he sort of guessed that in the war that was between Augusta and the Emperor of Jasper, that the ring of islands had just become a new rope in their eternal game of tug of war.

And that scared Charleston a lot more than he ever wanted to admit.

CHAPTER 5

Augusta watched wonderful Cargo flap his beautifully large blue wings as he returned to the ship, and she was waiting for him to tell her what the elves standing on the golden sandy beaches wanted them to do. She wasn't exactly sure if it was smart or not to send a dragon to talk to elves considering it was the elves that had caused them to flee into the human lands thousands of years ago, but he seemed okay thankfully.

She stood on the top deck of the flagship with the first-mate turning the wheel just enough for the ship to remain straight and heading towards the islands.

Augusta had to admit that now they were closer, the islands were absolutely stunning. She loved seeing how flat all the islands were, some were covered in golden sandy beaches, others were covered in small forests and others were made completely from stone.

The aroma of burnt ozone, charred flesh and gunpowder filled the air as black smoke veiled the sky in the distance so that had to be where the fighting was thickest, Augusta really wanted both elves and dwarfs to be in the mood for peace, but that wasn't likely.

Augusta hated how stubborn both races were towards each other. She hated the elves for their arrogance about magic and the dwarfs about their supremacy over craftsmanship.

Even though she always had believed that the elves were far better creators of stunning objects.

The sound of elves shouting in the distance made Augusta close her eyes, she had read up on elves for ages over the past 45 days and she really wanted to at least try to impress them. But she couldn't pick up any words. That was probably just because she had no clue where the words stopped and started as the elves were talking so quickly.

"Ya know," Cargo said as he reached the ship and hovered in front of Augusta for a moment, "those elves are sure fierce people. They thought I was a dwarfish attacker for a moment,"

Augusta's stomach twisted into a painful knot. She had written to the elves describing Cargo so they knew exactly *not* to attack him.

"Any good news?" Augusta asked.

"The elves want us to moor on the bay they're standing on then we will be escorted to Elven Command Island to meet the dwarfs,"

Augusta really didn't like the idea of that. From a diplomatic viewpoint it made a lot more sense to travel to a neutral location so both the dwarfs and elves knew they were equal partners in this peace.

She instantly knew that wasn't the case and the elves were not going to talk peace on equal terms with the dwarfs.

If she really had to name her favourite species before now, she had to admit that she was hoping the elves would align themselves with her if the other one wouldn't. But now she wasn't so sure.

Charleston folded his arms and she had actually forgotten he was there. "We have to play along for now,"

Augusta turned to the first mate. "Please do what Cargo says,"

The first mate nodded and then Augusta closed her eyes and focused on the dagger burn mark on her hand so she could secretly talk to Cargo.

And as he could read her thoughts, she really wanted him to go and ask the elves if they had captured the dwarf king for now, and if it was true then please don't hurt them.

Cargo's wonderful laughter echoed in her mind and he flew off.

Augusta really wasn't sure what she was expecting but if the elves had captured the dwarf monarch then peace was going to be next to impossible. She hated to imagine how happy Jasper would be with it though, it would give them the perfect opportunity to align themselves with the dwarfs against her kingdoms.

The dwarfs would never ever stop supplying

Jasper if the Emperor promised them revenge against the elves.

"Should I ready the troops?" a commander asked in bright golden uniform.

Augusta looked at Charleston. She wasn't sure what the best play here was.

"No thank you Commander," Charleston said. "The Queen and I will be fine travelling with the elves,"

Augusta smiled at the commander and hoped that Charleston had made the right call. The elves were very well known to be nobles at heart and they took their guests very seriously, so hopefully that applied to protection as well.

She almost laughed at herself because of how much hoping she was doing at the moment, but that was the problem with elves and dwarfs. They weren't human creatures, she knew how to handle humans but she had no experience with other species at all.

Augusta felt wonderful as Cargo reconnect with her mind and she bit her lip what the answer was even before Cargo spoke.

Ten iron pods churning out thick columns of smoke zoomed towards them and Augusta knew they were dwarfish warships.

The elves have the monarch.

Augusta just laughed because she had put herself right in the middle of a fight between the elves and dwarfs.

The dwarfs wanted their monarch back and

Augusta was fairly sure they would kill every single living thing that got in their way.

Including her, her people and the man she loved.

CHAPTER 6

Charleston flat out couldn't believe how stupid the elves were as he stepped off their small wooden boat that had taken them from the ship to the golden sandy beach. As much as he loved the hot sunshine, the wonderfully sweet-smelling air and the golden sand under his feet, Charleston was so not impressed with the elves.

Then he realised he was standing in front of a hundred of them. He was surprised all of them were wearing thin golden armour that was so beautiful with all its stunning patterns of trees, flowers and roots. It must have taken them years to forge a single piece of armour but Charleston knew that the elves were far too clever for that.

The elves all had sharp pointy ears, strong jawlines and their skin was beautiful. The women had to be some of the most beautiful ladies he had ever had the pleasure of seeing, and Augusta seemed fairly taken with the men as well.

Not that Charleston cared though because he could hardly judge.

The elves all raised their long perfectly handcrafted swords and shields with even more stunning patterns on them.

Then the elves raised their swords to their foreheads, said something in elvish and then rammed their swords into the ground.

Augusta bowed and Charleston did the same and Augusta started talking in very bad elvish that made some of the less mature elves laugh.

The elves bowed to Augusta and then one elf, a man in even more highly ornate armour than the others, rose up and walked straight up to Augusta.

Charleston forced himself not to react because this was clearly some sort of greeting that he didn't understand and he had to let it play out. He didn't dare let himself be the reason why this meeting failed and Jasper was allowed to conquer their three kingdoms.

Cannons roared in the distance and Charleston turned around.

He was amazed as a fleet of twenty long, elegant and beautiful elven warships glided through the crystal clear sea like it was nothing and zoomed towards the dwarfs.

The dwarfs fired cannon balls one after another and the balls simply melted before they hit the elven ships.

"Greeting Queen Augusta of Octogi, Lordigo

and Longmano. You are building quite an empire for yourself and I know you are here to get us to stop supporting Jasper. And yet there are greater reasons why the Will of the Islands bought you here," the elf said.

Charleston nodded. Because of everything and all the abuse had Owen had gone through he hated religion but the elves certainly made it more interesting and it was almost like Charleston could feel the magic in the very soil of the islands.

"Thank you mighty commander for greeting us in such an honourable way. When we return my crew has bought you wine, food and supplies as a gift for your generosity,"

The elf smiled but Charleston could tell it was a false smile.

"I appreciate that but I also know you seek to help the dwarfs and end the war. You are foolish your highness, these islands cannot be allowed to be inhibited. They will kill everyone on them in the end and I fear you will die simply by getting involved,"

Charleston had to admit the elf certainly knew how to sound crazy.

"My aims are to bring peace between the elves and dwarfs and to get you both to agree to weaken Jasper. He will conquer the whole world. I promise you I only seek to rule the human lands," Augusta said.

The commander nodded slowly. "Fine. You must come with me. I will take you to where we are holding the foul King of the Dwarfs. You might even witness his execution,"

Augusta stepped forward and all the elves shot up gripping their swords.

"If you kill the king then we cannot be allies. You will never have these islands and-"

The commander waved Augusta silent and Charleston placed his hands on his two swords.

"And nothing your highness. There is a lot to these islands you don't understand. I would hate to see your kingdom become leaderless because of your arrogance,"

Charleston wasn't sure who was winning on the arrogance front here. It certainly wasn't Augusta.

The commander clicked his fingers and as one all the soldiers stood at attention and created a path so the commander, Charleston and Augusta could walk through the golden sandy beaches of the island towards their destination.

Charleston kept his hands on both his swords. He just didn't trust these elves, he didn't believe what they were saying about the islands and he certainly didn't trust them to protect them if the dwarfs attacked.

And with the elves threatening to kill their monarch, Charleston would have been more surprised if they weren't attacked on the way there than if they were.

CHAPTER 7

For a species that apparently prided itself on being very quick, stealth and just perfect in every single way possible, Augusta was rather surprised that after two hours of walking through wonderfully warm golden sandy beaches, ankle-deep layers of bodies and a few islands covered in forests, that they were actually reaching their destination.

Smoke filled the horizon.

Augusta just shook her head as the elves that surrounded her like they were high-level targets for dwarfish assassins (they probably were) gasped as the row of dense trees ahead of them were burning.

In the past few hours she had learnt too much about elven strategy not to know that the immense tall, thick and deadly looking trees were meant to have elves hanging off them as a form of defence.

There were no elves hanging off these trees, they were no screams, no nothing.

The elves led her and Charleston who looked so

hot despite him sweating towards the line of trees.

The commander clicked his fingers and the flames were blown out like candles and that just concerned Augusta a lot more than she ever cared to admit because if the commander could do that so easily. Then why couldn't the elves at this base or whatever they called it do the same thing?

She followed the commander and Charleston into the smouldering remains of the trees and even the trees were charred and husks of their former glory, she was surprised that the trees were lining a grand circle.

The circle was covered in thick green grass that looked so beautiful except for the charred corpses of both elves and dwarfs. The corpses looked like they were fighting something that wasn't each other.

There were even pairs of elves and dwarves fighting back to back and that just confused the hell out of Augusta.

She had never ever heard of such a thing before and given how much hate the commander had spoken to the dwarfs when they were attacked twice in the past two hours, peace seemed impossible to both sides.

Until peace meant a chance at survival.

She hated to imagine what the hell could have caused elves and dwarfs not only to fight to defend each other, but also fought back-to-back. The fighting position that would have made it all too easy for one of them to kill the other.

That hadn't happened here.

The smell of charred corpses, burnt flesh and gunpowder filled the air and Augusta coughed it was so damn strong.

She stood in the middle of the circle and focused on a small fire that still burned on the far side of the circle and the commander was investigating it.

It still made no sense why all the other elves hadn't come through the trees and then again there were a hell of a lot of things that made no sense here. Augusta hated that there were so many questions.

Enemy movements incoming. Forty dwarfs.

Augusta sent loving thoughts towards Cargo and she told the commander but he didn't seem to care or listen. He was focusing way too much on that burning mark for her liking.

So she went over to him and Charleston joined her.

Augusta didn't understand what was so interesting about the mark considering it was just a human skull burning in the grass.

Then she realised that it wasn't burning the grass at all. This was some kind of magic that made sure the symbol or mark burned on forever without consuming any natural fuel for the fire.

"Can you do that?" the commander asked.

Augusta had no idea how the commander knew that she had small amounts of fire magic in her, but this was no time for lies, deception and foolish games.

"No," Augusta said. "I can make fires but not a

mark like this. But you know exactly what it is and you did hear me about the dwarfs right?"

"When they see this mark the war will be over," the commander said.

Augusta stumbled back and gripped Charleston's hand tight. It made no sense whatsoever that a mere mark could stop any entire war between two species that seriously hated each other.

And the way that the commander was so relaxed about it made no sense at all.

The air crackled with magical energy and the screams of elves filled the air and Augusta watched as blood red smoke veiled the sky from where she had left the elves.

She went to run towards them to help them fight but the commander gripped her arm so hard it hurt.

"They are dead," the commander said fighting back his rage. "I need those dwarfs here now,"

Augusta whipped out her sword. She hated the idea of the elves needing the dwarfs. Their sworn enemies.

Forty little dwarfs ran into the clearing wearing iron chainmail and they were so tiny Augusta thought they were hopping along the ground.

They all carried their hammers, tiny swords and one even carried a flame thrower and they bowed at each other.

Augusta just looked at the commander. "What the hell is going on here? You two aren't fighting. You're working together. Why?"

A deafening roar ripped through the circle and the commander whipped out his elven swords. They glowed bright blue.

"Your highness. If we survive this then I will tell you everything," he said.

As shadows flicked around the corners of her eyes she just nodded. She had to survive a battle with an enemy that she had no idea about.

She loved those odds.

CHAPTER 8

Charleston hated damn elves and bloody dwarves they were the worse people ever as he whipped out his two longswords. If they survived this damn battle then he was going to get answers about this even if he had to smash some skulls in.

No one dared to endanger beautiful Augusta.

All forty dwarves, the elven commander and the two humans stood back-to-back in the dead centre of the grass circle as immense black shadows danced around the charred trees.

Immense blood red smoke rose into the air and it zoomed towards them.

The black shadows disappeared and Charleston realised that the world was getting a lot darker. It was basically night time now and Charleston hated that. Just hated it.

"Here they come," the commander said.

The bloodred smoke curled around itself creating immense wolf-like creatures with snarling teeth, really long claws and toxic green breath that poured out of its nose like a chimney.

There were three of the wolves and Charleston really doubted they had the numbers to kill them.

The wolves charged.

Running straight at Charleston.

He swung.

His swords hit the smoke.

His swords shattered.

Pain shot up his arms.

Agony filled his hands.

He couldn't move them.

The nerves were damaged or something.

Augusta unleashed torrents of fire.

The wolf screamed.

It jumped at Augusta knocking her to the ground.

The commander grabbed Charleston.

He healed his hands.

The commander gave Charleston a dagger.

Charleston flew at the wolf.

Slashing at it.

The wolf howled in pain.

Charleston thrusted the dagger into the smoke.

The wolf screamed.

Augusta launched fireballs at it.

Again and again.

Charleston kept slashing at it.

He felt rage build in him.

He rammed the dagger into it.

So hard his hand fell into the creature.

Smoke engulfed Charleston.

He couldn't see anyone.

He screamed.

He saw faces in the smoke.

Owen. Augusta. Past loves.

All were screaming out his name for help.

They were dying.

Charleston couldn't help them.

A wolf danced around the smoke.

Eating everyone he loved.

The eating felt like someone was stabbing his brain.

Bright white blinding light engulfed him and Charleston's vision turned black.

"Charles," Augusta said clearly panicked and Charleston knew that the smoke and danger had to be gone from the circle but he still couldn't see.

"His sight will return shortly. I should have warned you both and for that I deeply say sorry to you humans,"

That had to be the damn elven commander.

"What these two hummies doing in these parts laddie?"

Charleston just shook his head that had to be some kind of dwarf. Bloody short idiots.

"We were here to help you two negotiate peace and I was hoping you two could kindly stop trading with Jasper. We need to weaken them before they kill all of us," Augusta said. "But clearly you two are up to something,"

The dwarf laughed and Charleston so badly wanted to see but only small rays of light were returning to him.

"Well missy I have to admit I ain't thrilled about stopping trade but the pointy ears say your kingdom is trustworthy and your conquest will stop with the human lands. I trust the pointy ears so I trust you,"

These had to be the weirdest creatures Charleston had ever met.

Charleston felt a very soft and light hand touch his shoulder so he was guessing the commander was touching him.

"The elves and dwarves will agree to whatever you want if you can help us with our problem,"

Charleston's sight returned in such a flash that he staggered backwards as the daylight and warm sunshine was quite a shock.

Charleston was surprised that a very short dwarf waring gold chainmail was standing in front of him carrying two hammers.

"The name is Glumpy," the dwarf said. "I'm the sonny of the King and it was my idea to let ya come to these wee parts,"

Charleston just nodded. "Thank you,"

"Ah don't mention it. Ya probably going to die here anyway,"

Charleston and Augusta laughed but he seriously hoped the dwarf wasn't right.

"What the hell is going on?" Charleston asked.

The commander nodded. "We need to fake a war between our cultures because there's a group of humans working for your Jasper that is hunting us down. The Elven Empire is very scared of an attack, the dwarves have already lost ten mines to them,"

"And one of them contained ma best hammer. I lost my bloody hammer," Glumpy said.

"We know a lot more about human affairs than you will ever know," the commander said. "And because of that we will align ourselves with both of you but we cannot do anything to help you until these humans are dealt with,"

Charleston pointed to the charred trees. "If the humans did that then what the hell attacked us just now?"

Glumpy frowned. "That's a reason laddie why the elves are so depressing about this wee place. There are imprisoned creatures here that seek to kill the world and those damn humans are awakening them,"

Charleston nodded. "The humans are weaponizing these creatures against you,"

"I presume Jasper has already sent a ship to collect this group and the creatures," Augusta said.

"Correct your highness," the commander said. "There is a massive Jasper fleet of ships coming in two days to collect the humans. When a creature is released the person who did the deed becomes its master,"

Charleston smiled at the woman he loved and he

really loved how wide her eyes were because she must have realised the same opportunity as him.

"If a sizeable chunk of Jasper's navy comes here and we destroy it," Charleston said. "Then that will really weaken them,"

The commander and the dwarf looked at each other.

Glumpy hopped up and down for a moment until Charleston realised that he was actually pacing on the spot. He was so small it was hard to tell.

"If you hummies and you pointy deal with the humans. Me and me peeps could create a type of naval defence,"

Charleston stepped forward. "Please use our flagship too. It is at your disposal,"

August nodded.

"Ha. Hummies thinking their engineering is better than dwarfs. Classic. I look forward to it getting blown up,"

Charleston was about to say something as Glumpy and the remaining ten dwarfs ran away but again they still looked like they were hopping about like little children.

Augusta folded her arms and looked at the commander. "Who are you?"

Charleston nodded. That was a good question.

The commander grinned. "My name is Danlas, Lord Commander of the Elven army, King of the Elven Empire and Husband of the Mother Of Light,"

Charleston just frowned. The very last thing he

needed was to be surrounded by two monarchs. One was bad enough even if he loved her.

CHAPTER 9

Augusta was absolutely honoured to be in the presence of such a great monarch, she had heard a few stories about the wonderful King of the Elves and she had to admit he was a great warrior, probably the best she had ever seen.

Augusta stood in front of three black perfect cubes of stone that had a slight shine to them, and despite the harsh weather conditions in this section of the ring of islands. There wasn't a single chip on them, sign of weathering and they just looked so weird.

She at least expected there to be a sign of them being affected by the tide as it was clear by the layer of green seaweed on the ground of the island that it would be affected by the tide.

But the more Augusta looked at it, the more she realised the seaweed stopped just short of touching the cubes. And the air felt weird here, it felt thicker and more magically charged to the normal air so much so that it sort of felt like she was walking in water.

The sound of seagulls and Cargo overhead made her smile. She waved at her wonderful dragon and Cargo flew down to see her.

His large dragon paws landed in the water and a slight humming sound came from the cubes.

Danlas frowned. "These are what the humans are after. These are what we called… um, I think it translates to Soul Balls in your tongue,"

Augusta nodded. "These are empty I presume. The humans already own the creatures inside these cubes. So how many are there?"

Charleston tapped on each of the cubes and Danlas frowned at him like he was some annoying child who couldn't be left alone.

"There are over fifty of these black stone objects of all different sizes, shapes and textures in the ring of islands. The humans have claimed all of them except the most powerful and dangerous creature," Danlas said.

Augusta went over to Cargo and brushed his snout as Danlas continued.

"The Angel of Death is actually an old elven goddess that was defeated two thousand years ago when she went rogue. She became a killer for hire and she murdered so many innocent elves in a single night,"

"Until Danlas, the King of the Elven Gods, captured her and casted her away into the darkness of a Soul Ball," Augusta said. "Yes, my mother read the stories to me and my brother when we were children,"

"A great woman," Danlas said bowing.

Augusta did the same and she went back to the cubes. It was clear they weren't natural at all and the stone was weird.

When she placed her hand on the cube, palm down, an image of a snarling bloodred bear appeared looking at her like she was a tasty meal. And then the bear changed to one becoming scared.

Augusta backed away slowly and then went over to another cube.

A hungry image of a massive raven appeared and it came towards her but then it backed away.

The exact same thing happened to the wolf that appeared in her mind.

"These creatures are scared of me," Augusta said.

Danlas shook his head. "No my friend. They are scared of your magic and that is why I gave Charleston an elven dagger. A magic weapon in its own right and something that can kill these foul creations,"

"Magic harms magic," Augusta said as she remembered she had read in the books that belonged to her old Chief Witch before she turned traitor.

"How do we find this Angel of Death?" Augusta asked.

Danlos shrugged. Clearly not having a clue. "All the objects seem random,"

"There is no such thing as random when it comes to magic," Augusta said quoting something else from her traitorous Witch's books.

Dark shadows appeared in the corners of her eyes but when she looked about she couldn't see anything. Judging by the looks on Charleston's and Danlas's face they had seen it too.

"The enemy will be here soon,"

"Not if we don't kill you first," a male human said.

Augusta spun around and waved Cargo not to kill the twenty human males walking towards them wearing orange robes and their faces were covered in bright orange wrapping so she couldn't even see their eyes.

They were carrying glowing red swords that had to contain the creatures. Why didn't they release them yet and just kill them?

"Oh, the Queen will love to see this one," a man said looking at Augusta.

All the humans appeared to nod and all three of them whipped out their swords.

Cargo opened his mouth to roar but Augusta actually felt like going with these people. She had to learn exactly what was going on here and she doubted even Danlas knew what was happening.

"How about a trade?" Augusta said. "I go with you and you allow my friends to live,"

The humans cocked their heads and Charleston just looked at her. She blew him a kiss.

"I can find out information," she said.

"But you might get hurt,"

Augusta laughed. "My death is nothing if you get to live and find this Angel of Death before they do and remember the *dagger*,"

Augusta subtly showed him the burn mark on her hand Charleston weakly smiled. At least Cargo would still be able to read her thoughts and she could give him information to tell the others.

"We except and we promise not to kill your friends this time," someone said.

Augusta went over to them and looked at Charleston just in case something went wrong. He was so beautiful, handsome and perfect.

"I love you," she said.

"Me too," Charleston said.

As heavy hands gripped Augusta's arms she didn't hesitate or anything, she simply allowed the men to take her away.

And Augusta focused on the fact that she was doing this to protect her people, her kingdoms and most importantly the man she loved.

CHAPTER 10

As much as Charleston loved his beautiful, sexy lover, he really didn't want Augusta to be with those damn humans any more than she had to be. Thankfully Cargo had confirmed every single time he asked (which was a lot according to the dragon) that she was okay or at least still alive.

That was hardly reassuring.

But when Augusta had mentioned that nothing was random with magic, Charleston just got the really strong urge to see a map of the ring of islands, and he knew the elves a little too well to know that they had to have a map.

His father had loved elven maps because they were always works of art, soft and very accurate. Far more accurate than any maps created by a human hand.

Charleston went into the large elven encampment that Danlas had led him too and it was certainly stunning. The soft golden sand moved under his feet lovingly and like the sand itself wanted, needed to support him.

The large encampment had tens, maybe a hundred little tents made out of trees, bushes and other wonderful delights that made the tents look like they were natural and belonged there. It was so typical of the elves to work with the environment instead of bending it and forcing it to do whatever they wanted. Charleston really wished humans learnt that lesson too.

Groups of elves were sitting on wonderful wooden benches that grew out of the ground as they sang amazing songs that were so relaxing to the ear, they were chatting about the battles they had fought in and they were eating something rather stunning.

Charleston had no idea what it actually was but it looked like some kind of rich fruity stew with no meat in it, and it all looked perfectly natural.

"It is called, in your tongue, *Plentiful Stew*. We elves magic up the fruit and vegetables and other ingredients from the ground and make it whenever we need it most," Danlas said.

Then Charleston realised that there was a large burnt patch of golden sand that was now blackened and he assumed that was where the elven supplies once were. Including their own food and water supplies.

"Please," Danlas said. "This way,"

Charleston followed Danlas past the elves that smiled, waved and cheered at him like he was already some kind of war hero. Maybe he was to them given how much the elves seemed to know about their culture and Augusta's plan for conquest.

Charleston went into a small tree-made tent with fireflies flying about creating more than enough light to see where he was going and he could probably read in this light it was that good. He was even surprised at the wonderful smell of strawberries.

He went over to a large oak table that looked magical and Danlas tapped it three times and a map formed.

Charleston was stunned at how beautiful it was. The map was certainly to scale and it was even three-dimensional. He could see all the islands spread out over the ring and even troop movements.

There was a large band of humans in the far south of the ring of islands and Charleston was currently in the central regions towards the east. He didn't really like being that close to the group of humans attacking them.

"What did you want to inspect?" Danlas asked.

Charleston leant on the table and checked to see if Danlas was frowning at him, which he thankfully wasn't.

"Augusta mentioned that nothing is random with magic so I don't believe the placement of these stones are either,"

Danlas nodded and tapped on the table again.

A second later, all the locations of black stones found so far appeared on the map. It was stunning to see that most if not all the islands had creatures on them.

"Please forgive me my friend, I did not tell you the whole truth when I revealed the purpose of these islands. There are far more creatures than I told you about and the humans have them all,"

Charleston shook his head. There had to be easily a hundred or more creatures in the hands of the group of humans.

"Please tell me there's a weakness," he said.

Danlas didn't dare look at him. "We are working on it,"

Charleston wanted to swear or something because Augusta was literally walking into a death trap all because the elves had withheld information.

Charleston was about to complain to Danlas but he noticed that as stupid as it sounded there wasn't a single black stone marked on the central islands.

Of course, all the islands were designed in a ring shape but there were four islands in the middle of it all. No one had explored them yet.

He looked at Danlas. "We need to go to the central islands,"

"Impossible. Those waters dissolve all flesh, bone and ships that I have sent already. There are no monsters because the water itself is so toxic,"

Charleston grinned. "But you forget we have a dragon on our side,"

Danlas slowly and very elegantly nodded. "I will get us a group of soldiers,"

"And then we march on the central islands,"

CHAPTER 11

Augusta was seriously not impressed as the group of humans escorting her to the awful leader of theirs that called herself Queen, led her into their headquarters.

It was hardly a headquarters to be honest and Augusta was so looking forward to escaping from here. This was a really bad idea after all.

The headquarters was on an oval-shaped island covered in thick palm trees with golden, red and blue flowers blowing in the warm wind and there were tons of humans wrapped up in orange robes. And all of them had their faces wrapped up even tighter in orange cloth.

That was just strange and Augusta really hated these humans more than anything in the entire world. It was so unnatural not to see the face of another human, but they all stopped what they were doing on the island and came towards her.

Augusta was still relieved they had allowed her to

keep her sword but she forced herself not to reach for it. She had a weird feeling that she wasn't in danger yet.

Tens upon tens of orange robed humans lined up to create a perfect path for Augusta towards a large white tent made from the finest silk. But then she realised that it wasn't silk at all.

It was elven skin.

Augusta gulped as she felt a gentle touch on her lower back that pushed her onwards.

Augusta kept walking and she went inside the white silk tent and there was nothing inside it except a bronze throne with a woman sitting on it, three elven slaves and a cross with fresh blood on it.

The woman on the throne was completely naked with tribal markings painted on her skin and she just looked at Augusta like she was nothing more than a mere object of curiosity, like how a cat might look at a piece of string before attacking it.

"Queen Augusta of Octogi, Lordigo and Longmano. The Emperor warned me about you but he did not expect you to be here so quickly," the woman said.

Augusta wanted to look away from the body because her lady features were basically eye-level because of the throne's height but Augusta's damn regal training forced her to keep looking.

"I am not your enemy but I plead with you to stop this hunt for Jasper. If you surrender now and free the elves then you can be free of Jasper's influence," Augusta said.

The woman laughed and she swirled her hand.

Moments later five orange-robed men walked into the tent and they started undoing their robes and when they dropped Augusta was expecting to see more naked bodies but she didn't.

All she saw was dust crumble away and she instantly knew that all these humans had been turned to dust and it was only the robes and wrappings that contained their soul or life force or whatever people called it.

"Jasper has control of us whatever happens. You are a threat to us and if I fail then the Emperor will turn me into one of those mindless drones," the woman said.

Augusta nodded and as much as she wanted to use the woman's fear against her, she was a lot more concerned at the idea that the Emperor of Jasper could actually do such powerful magic.

The last thing she wanted was to send her forces into Jasper to conquer it only for them to be turned into mindless drones for her enemy.

She couldn't have that.

Augusta focused on the dagger burn mark on her hand and sent all this information to Cargo.

"What would it take for you to work with me and not against me?" Augusta asked.

The woman shook her head and she actually looked so hopeless. "There is nothing in the world that could free me. All these people in robes were my clan, my friends, my family, my lovers,"

Augusta nodded. "You're Victoria Snatcher, Chieftain of Jasper Raiders,"

The woman smiled weakly. "That was a very long time ago,"

Augusta felt so pleased to be in the presence of such a wonderful, brilliant and brutal warrior but the woman she had read about since she was a child was clearly gone or something.

The Jasper Raiders were a brilliant tribe that had stolen millions of coins and supplies from Jasper and all over the human lands to give to the poor. Thankfully they never really touched Octogi because she always loved her people, but the kingdoms were heavily targeted.

Clearly the Emperor had captured them once and imprisoned them.

"What if the elves can save you?" Augusta asked.

The woman shot up and stomped her feet on the ground. "Enough of this rubbish,"

Augusta felt tens of hands grip her arms.

"I have had enough talking and lectures from the likes of you. Men, women take her to the central islands and sacrifice her to the Angel of Death. Once she is filled she can be unleashed on the world,"

Augusta hated the sound of that.

"And," the woman said, "then the Angel of Death can kill all the humans including Jasper, the elves and the dwarfs. I want to wipe this world clean,"

CHAPTER 12

As Charleston slipped off Cargo's shiny and perfectly smooth blue scales, he really didn't feel like he could ever come to enjoy travelling by dragon like Augusta seemingly loved too. But he did love Cargo nonetheless, he was a great, kind and very sociable dragon.

He was surprised at the sheer hardness of the granite island and these four central regions were completely different to other islands in the ring. Even the air was different with it being so thick that it felt like he was walking around in a thick soup.

All his movements seemed slow, strange and like he couldn't possibly do anything too quick on these islands, so clearly there was some kind of powerful magic at work here. And Charleston really hated magic working against him.

Charleston looked out around the massive moat of steaming, bubbling and sulfur stinking water and he was just surprised at how immense the distance was. He knew that the ring of islands was massive but he could barely see the golden sandy beaches of the closest islands that lined the edge of the moat.

Whoever had created the ring of islands really didn't want these central islands to be touched, and as Charleston walked on them he couldn't help but realise that the ground felt alive.

The ground looked hard, solid and unbreakable but as he walked he felt the rock soften around his feet as if the rock itself was testing what he was.

Cargo looked like he was about to step onto the island but he waved him away.

"No," he said. "You cannot come on here Cargo. I think, I think the island is sensitive to organic matter,"

Danlas nodded. "We must endeavour to keep our shoes on. I have seen this magic before and if it detects flesh then the magic will devour us,"

Charleston slowly turned around despite him wanting to move as quickly as possible on these islands, but then he noticed how all the islands were now one single large one made from solid black granite. The change had to be quick and it was so weird.

All Charleston wanted to do was get away from the island but they had to stop the group of humans.

"The orange wrapped people are all dust," Cargo said as he explained every little detail that Augusta had sent him about her meeting with their so-called Queen.

Charleston nodded. It was so much to take in, he had fought the Jasper Raiders at least five times over the last few years because they were so good at raiding Lordigo. They were always pain in the asses but that was life, and Charleston hated killing them because they were giving to the poor but he had to defend his kingdom.

Now Charleston wasn't so sure he should have. Maybe this situation would have played out very differently or maybe he wouldn't have ever met beautiful Augusta.

He shivered at the very notion of never meeting the woman he loved.

The horror.

"The magic is constantly changing here and look at these burn marks," Danlas said.

Charleston went over to him and noticed that at the base of a large granite pillar that radiated icy coldness were black charring marks.

"These burn marks are not from the outside. These marks are from the Angel of Death trying to escape," Danlas said.

Charleston had no idea how the hell that was possible. It shouldn't be. From everything the elves had told him about this place, they were the first ever to touch it and walk on it and the Angel was meant to be weak and defeated.

How the hell could a weak Angel create magical fire?

Charleston took a step forward and fell

midstride.

It was so weird that he hadn't realised his body must have corrected for the strange slow-moving magic but it was now gone. Charleston could move normally.

"Guys," Cargo said.

Charleston spun around and bit his lip as he saw three massive bloodred snakes were swimming towards them with ten or twenty orange-wrapped men and women and Augusta was on the back of them.

Charleston looked at Cargo. "Leave us. Stay local though. We will need a quick escape,"

He was surprised that Cargo looked at Danlas for approval as if his plan was crazy and it probably was but he didn't protest.

Cargo nodded and then flew away quickly just as the snakes reached the black granite shore and everyone stepped off.

Augusta ran to Charleston but the orange humans grabbed her and pressed her body against the black stone pillar.

Charleston was about to charge at the enemy but Danlas gripped his arm tight.

"Do not save her yet. We have to learn first," he said.

Charleston just bit his lip because if Augusta got hurt or died then he wouldn't rest until every single elf and dwarf on this ring of islands was dead.

Very dead.

CHAPTER 13

The large black stone pillar burnt icy coldness in Augusta's back as she was pressed into it by the foul orange humans. She tried to struggle but she couldn't and she felt small pieces of magical ice crystals form over the top of her skin.

Augusta felt like she was being watched, inspected and touched up by someone or something that most certainly was not human. She hated the air as it was filled with the foul smell of rusty metal and the taste of iron formed on her tongue.

All she wanted was to escape but Augusta really hated these humans, the strange water and the strange islands that housed the Angel of Death.

Despite Augusta's vision starting to go weird and she hated that even more, she heard the foul humans talk about the Angel of Death getting a feast but she couldn't understand why Charleston wasn't doing anything.

Maybe he was. She had seen Cargo fly away

moments before she reached the islands so maybe he was escaping to get reinforcements.

"I have heard of creatures like you," a woman said.

Augusta looked around and saw a woman in black robes, ash pouring off her skin where a face should have been and a thin veil covering her dust face was a horrible sight.

The veil was thin and very well-worn like it had been worn for tens of thousands of years but that was impossible considering this had to be the Angel of Death and she hadn't been in here for more than two thousand years.

The Angel gestured towards the orange humans as they spoke but Augusta couldn't hear the words and she felt how scared Charleston was.

"I was rather looking forward to getting a royal sacrifice at some point. I thought it would be the stupid elves that freed me. I thought the dwarves might be smart enough to do some point. But nope, I can always rely on the stupidity of humans to free little old me,"

Augusta just looked at the woman. "I will not be a willing sacrifice,"

The Angel laughed. "You think, wow, you actually think this is about willingness. Willingness don't mean shit to me your highness, the more unwilling the sacrifice the more powerful it is,"

Do you need help?

Augusta hissed as Cargo's words of kindness

entered her mind but the Angel looked up at the sky like she had heard them.

Augusta couldn't see her face but she knew that the Angel was smiling.

"A dragon. Now that is a new one. A dragon connected to a human now that is even newer. Just imagine the power I could have if I was a dragon and inside its body,"

Augusta tried to move but her body was covered in large blocks of ice.

"Charleston!" she shouted but it didn't look like anyone could hear her.

"Pathetic you humans. Now let me see the mark," the Angel said coming over to Augusta.

Augusta knew if the Angel touched her then she would die so she had to make a very deadly choice. She could show the dagger mark to the Angel and sacrifice Cargo or she could let the Angel touch her hand and it would kill her.

Augusta hated the damn choice. Either one would damn Cargo but either way, because of how the dragon connection worked if Cargo died then Augusta basically got another life.

She hated how this silly magic worked.

Augusta moved her hand and the ice melted away and she extended her fingers revealing the Angel to clearly see the dagger burn mark on her palm.

"Forgive me my love," Augusta said to Cargo.
Always.

"I hope you enjoy knowing you have damned

your entire world to die. And I will start off by killing the Victoria woman," the Angel said.

Augusta screamed as crippling pain filled her as the Angel of Death flew into her dagger burn mark and it glowed bright black as the Angel flew into the depths of Cargo's mind.

The pain grew even worse as Cargo's life force flew into her veins, body and mind and her eyes bungled and twisted as she couldn't handle this new power.

She felt Charleston and Danlas grab her as she realised she could make sound once more.

"Kill me," Augusta said.

"Kill an orange thing now," Danlas said. "Get me some wrappings,"

Augusta felt blood pour down her nose. Her eyes felt like they were about to pop.

Augusta heard a scream and then she felt Danlas wrap some of the orange wrapping around her chest and then he spoke rapid elvish.

And she felt normal again and she took the small piece of orange cloth that glowed white and Danlas smiled at her.

"The life force of your dragon is here in the cloth. If the cloth gets destroyed then your dragon is gone forever,"

Augusta nodded and she tucked the cloth into the bottom of her boot so there was no chance of losing it.

The loud deafening sound of a dragon roaring

echoed around the ring of islands and Augusta just shook her head as Cargo's scales were no longer blue, they were blackened, charred and flaky.

The Angel of Death had just murdered her best friend and now Augusta had to get revenge and hopefully restore her friend.

But as much as she hated to admit it, that was impossible without the help of the Jasper Raiders.

And that meant Augusta needed Victoria very much alive.

CHAPTER 14

Charleston seriously hadn't expected this trip to go this badly and have this many twists and turns, it was a nightmare and he really didn't want the trip to keep going this badly.

He hated the foul headquarters of the Jasper Raiders with their little tents and large palm trees flapping like flags in the wind, and the hard rocks under his feet.

He whipped out his two swords that almost blinded him at first because of the angle of the light as it struck the blades but then the sky turned dark as the Angel had come for them.

The Angel-dragon roared in fury as it flew at them.

Charleston leapt to one side.

Augusta raised her swords. She froze.

She couldn't strike Cargo's body.

Charleston tackled her to the ground.

Immense torrents of black flames shot down.

Orange humans stormed out of the tree line and tents.

They whipped out spears. Swords. Hammers.

They threw them at the Angel.

The Angel launched fireballs at them.

Melting the weapons instantly.

Charleston charged at the Angel as it flew low over the headquarters.

He jumped up.

Swung his swords.

The swords did nothing.

He threw the swords at Cargo's body.

They bounced off.

Charleston whipped out the dagger Danlas had given him.

Charleston flew at the Angel.

Jumping into the air.

Danlas joined him.

Augusta unleashed a torrent of blue flame.

The Angel screamed as they swung their blades.

They ripped into Cargo's flesh.

The Angel scream grew even louder.

Then it turned into a laugh and everyone instantly stopped as the wounds healed themselves and the Angel simply floated there in the middle of the island, and it focused on the tent that had naked Victoria coming out from it.

The Queen roared in utter fury as was so common for her people to do but Charleston knew even her rage and brutality was no match for the dragon.

Charleston went over to Augusta and Danlas. "We have to leave now,"

Danlas looked at him and shook his head. "I have the magical knowledge to restore these dust people to flesh and blood. But I need time,"

Augusta looked at him. "How much?"

"As much as you can give me,"

Charleston blew a kiss at the woman he loved and she actually came over and kissed his cheek.

"Oi lumpy," Charleston shouted at the Angel.

The Angel flapped her wings in a very strange fashion like she was still getting used to invading Cargo's body.

"You are nothing but a weak pathetic Angel," Augusta said. "You really think a real Goddess would allow herself to be captured?"

The Angel grinned at her.

Charleston stepped forward. "I mean if I were the other gods and goddesses, I would think that goddess wasn't even worthy of the name. I think you're a dwarf at best,"

The Angel spat and looked in utter horror at the insult. Clearly she believed being a dwarf was the lowest of the low.

"You know my love," Charleston said. "I think every single dwarf on these islands is smarter than this so-called Angel of Death. Or more likely lard-ass of Death,"

Charleston was surprised steam poured out of

the Angel's ears and her throat glowed white hot.

She roared.

Charleston tackled Augusta.

Augusta stepped away.

Grabbing Charleston and they ran to one side.

They kept running.

Diving behind some trees.

And landing in some bushes.

The Angel didn't stop breathing fire until everyone was a crispy, smouldering corpse.

Charleston felt his eyes turn watery as he spotted the smouldering corpse of Danlas, Victoria and every single Jasper Raider that they had just tried to save.

They had just basically killed everyone they were trying to save.

CHAPTER 15

Charleston was seriously not impressed with the stupid dwarves as he stood on the golden sandy beach of the outer most island in the ring, and watched as all the dwarves sped off in their speedboats towards their iron pod-like ships.

They were going to escape and say that the mission was complete, safe and the threat was no more. Charleston had no idea how the hell Glumpy was going to lie to the Dwarfian King and the Elves when he returned, but he was clearly going to.

Charleston hated it even more how the Cargo's possessed body flew around in circles high above them, and Augusta just frowned more and more as the dragon she had once loved was now going to kill them.

Charleston still had no idea why the Angel of Death wasn't attacking them considering they were sitting ducks watching most of the dwarfs leave, since Glumpy was still on the beach pushing off the other speedboats.

That concerned him a lot more than he ever wanted to admit.

Augusta stepped towards Glumpy. "You cannot leave this battle yet. The Elven King is dead. Don't you feel any loyalty to him and getting revenge,"

Glumpy chuckled. "Of course I do lassie, but I ain't gonna struggle and die here when I can go home, eat fatty food and drink me ale,"

Charleston couldn't believe the dwarves were that stupid and cowards at heart, he had always admired the dwarves slightly but now he just wanted them gone. They were useless and if the Angel of Death really was going to kill everything on the planet, then he was just hoping she would start with the dwarves.

Charleston gasped when he saw twenty elegant wooden ships that looked like blades slicing through the water, elven ships, and he was horrified that even the elves were leaving.

Of course Augusta had told a slightly diplomatic story about how Danlas had tried to save everyone and that was why he died. Neither of them dared to tell the elves it was their taunting that had gotten everyone killed.

Something that still killed him inside.

"Thank you for your help," an elf said as he walked on top of the sand and not sinking unlike Charleston.

Augusta didn't say anything so Charleston didn't

either.

"You can both rest assured that the elves and dwarves will no longer supply evil Jasper and our ships will arrive in your docks in four months' time. You will have our help conquering Jasper," the elf said.

Augusta smiled, bowed and placed her sword to her forehead which the elf seemed to think was funny.

Then the elf did the same and he started swimming towards his ship a few miles away.

"So we have no Dwarfian friends, no elves and no nothing to help us defeat the Angel," Charleston said.

Augusta smiled. "We've certainly had easier fights. We don't even have a dragon to help us,"

Charleston was about to say something when Augusta hissed in pain and started hopping about like there was a nail pressing into her foot.

She quickly whipped off her boot and Charleston grinned when he saw she was holding the small piece of orange cloth containing Cargo's lifeforce.

A loud roar screamed overhead but Charleston's stomach twist into a painful knot. It was only a matter of time before the Angel of Death attacked them now that the elves and dwarfs were fleeing.

And as much as Charleston wanted to be happy about Jasper no longer getting supplies and would be really weakened with them and their Jasper Raider allies, he really didn't.

Augusta came over to him and Glumpy even came over and laughed.

"Come on lassie that dragon cannot be in there forever. You better get that dragon into a body before it, goes away," he said.

Charleston shook his head as Glumpy laughed away to him and muttered something about how much he was looking forward to having fried chicken, ale and more ale.

Glumpy hopped on the last speedboat on the beach and he zoomed away.

"We could use some help!" Augusta shouted.

No one listened. No one cared. No one wanted to help them because the elves and the dwarves clearly didn't believe this was their fight.

Charleston took beautiful Augusta by the hand and they started walking down the wonderful golden sandy beach towards the flagship that was a few islands over.

If they could get back to the ship, their last line of defence and place filled with allies, then maybe they could create a plan to save everyone.

"Oh look," Augusta said.

Charleston waved as the immense flagship with the first mate at the steering wheel (Charleston really had to find out what that was called at some point) zoomed towards them.

A loud roar filled the air.

Charleston looked up.

The Angel of Death was zooming towards the

ship.

Charleston didn't have anything to hand.

Augusta unleashed fireballs at the Angel.

The Angel kept zooming.

Bells screamed out on the flagship.

Charleston gasped as the Angel smashed into the flagship.

It exploded.

Hundreds of little flaming bodies popped out.

Within moments the flagship crumbled under its own annihilated weight and the Angel of Death just laughed as she flew away.

Charleston just hugged the woman he loved because they had just lost their last hope of soldiers, allies and intelligent minds to help them come up with a plan to defeat the Angel.

They were alone. Well and truly alone.

CHAPTER 16

Augusta just slumped to the ground as she saw the flaming wreckage of her mighty flagship. The wonderful symbol of her power, her might and everything she wanted her growing Empire to be and she hated it. She bloody hated the Angel of Death.

All Augusta wanted was to cry or scream or shout but she sadly knew that wouldn't matter here. She was normally such a strong leader but even then her kingdom was typically only a day or two away.

Her kingdom, her allies, her friends were months away but then she would be dead.

She just sunk her hands into the piping hot golden sand of the beach and she focused on the painful, burning sensation in case there was some kind of answer in the pain, but to be honest she just wanted to feel something other than pain for a single moment.

It was all her stupid fault that Danlas, the elves and dwarves and now her own wonderful people were dead. Hell even her best friend in the entire world was possessed or something.

She was a failure.

But she also knew that a person was only a failure if they ever dared to allow those moments of weakness to define them and become their life.

Augusta wasn't a failure so she forced herself up and she took the wonderfully rough, manly hands of the man she loved.

"Our mission is simple," Augusta said. "We have to somehow stop the Angel of Death, restore Cargo and escape this place alive,"

Charleston kissed her gently on the cheek. "I think that orange piece of cloth is the key,"

"What? You think because the Angel kicked out Cargo in the first place that Cargo could kick her out?"

Charleston nodded and Augusta jumped as the orange piece of cloth burned a little in her loose grip. She took that as a yes.

"And then," Charleston said, "think about how vulnerable you were after Cargo was kicked out. If the Angel ends up like that then we should be able to kill her,"

Augusta really liked that plan but they would have to be careful, stealthy and they would actually have to combine all the skills that elves, dwarves and humans had.

"Okay," she said. "We will have to be as brutal as humans, as loud and chaotic as dwarves and as silent and quick as elves,"

Charleston laughed. "Not a lot then for two mere humans,"

"That's why I love you Charles. A man of many talents even outside the bedroom,"

Augusta laughed as Charleston gave her a mocking bow. And Augusta looked around to see if this beach would be open enough for them to attack the Angel.

Then she realised that somewhere with dense trees would be better.

"Come then. Let's go and try not to die," Augusta said.

Charleston hesitated for a moment before following her. "Death is certain. We have no friends, no allies and even the dwarves and elves know this is impossible,"

Augusta just hugged him because if they were both going to die then Charleston was definitely the man she wanted to die fighting aside.

"Come on laddie. Us dwarves we like a bit of a challenge. It makes the ales better even better afterwards," Glumpy said as he hopped off his speedboat with a handful of dwarves.

"And us elves like a challenge," the male elf from earlier said as him and five female elven archers appeared out of nowhere.

Augusta smiled because these people really were amazing. She was fairly willing to bet that they had never actually left and they were only checking if

Augusta and Charleston had the determination to defeat the Angel.

"Come on. We have an Angel to kill," Augusta said.

"Right you are lassie,"

CHAPTER 17

Charleston felt so excited about their rather bad plan of attacking the Angel of Death just enough to allow Augusta to get close enough to Cargo's body to kick out the Angel.

The six elves were hiding somewhere in the thick beautiful palm trees that lined the outside of the oval island they were on, the sound of waves smashing into the white sandy beach was a little unnerving and the group of little dwarves around Charleston in the middle of the lush green grass was tense.

Augusta was standing a few metres from him and she looked determined.

Charleston so badly didn't want her to get hurt.

"Lard-ass of death!" Augusta shouted.

Charleston smiled at the insult but as the immense deafening flapping of wings ripped through the air his stomach tensed.

Thankfully the oval island was far too small for Cargo to land on but he had a feeling that didn't matter for the Angel.

The Angel roared overhead.

She smashed down trees.

Charleston spun around.

The Angel was heading straight for them.

He leapt to one side.

The dwarves were too slow.

They swung their arms.

The Angel laughed.

She chomped down on them.

Cargo hissed.

Dragon teeth were smashed out.

The dwarves were still alive.

Charleston whipped out the elven dagger.

He charged over to the Angel.

She was still flying about.

Charleston couldn't reach her.

Cargo's front teeth were shattered.

Little dwarves jumped out the opening.

Augusta unleashed torrents of white flame at the Angel.

Again and again.

Charleston charged forward.

The Angel was flying lower.

She looked pained.

Charleston leapt into the air.

Swinging his dagger.

It sliced into Cargo.

The Angel screamed.

It roared.

Unleashing torrents of black fire.

Charleston tackled Augusta.

They both leapt up.

A torrent was shooting towards them.

Augusta thrusted out her hands.

A white torrent shot out of them.

The Angel grinned as the torrents met.

Charleston charged towards the Angel.

She flapped Cargo's wings.

Knocking him backwards.

Augusta wasn't strong enough.

Her torrent couldn't withstand the Angel's.

Charleston tackled her to one side.

The black torrent smashed into where she was standing.

Dwarves threw potions. Hammers. Everything at the dragon.

Charleston didn't know why the elves weren't attacking.

An Elven horn roared out.

Everyone stopped as no one had any idea why the hell an elf would unleash their war cry and then Augusta pulled him to the ground.

Seconds later cannon balls ripped through the air.

The Angel spat out fireballs and melted them.

The Angel spat out even stronger fireballs.

Charleston heard the ships explode in the distance.

Six elves charged out of the trees.

Charleston charged towards The Angel.

She spun around.

Smashing her tail into them.

Killing all six elves.

Their corpses splattered a few metres away.

Augusta shot out her hands again. Creating immense fiery rope. Wrapping it around Cargo's feet.

Charleston flew at the Angel as Augusta lowered it.

The Angel looked panicked.

The dwarves ran with him.

The Angel flapped her wings as much as she could.

Augusta screamed.

Flying up into the air.

The Angel shook her free.

Charleston caught Augusta as she flew.

The Angel flapped her wings.

Creating a hurricane.

Knocking everyone to the ground.

Charleston felt all the energy, determination and rage inside him was defeated and gone but he just focused on beautiful Augusta as she forced herself up holding her right side.

Charleston forced himself up to.

"You cannot defeat me," the Angel said. "The elves are gone. All the dwarves but Glumpy are dead. And now you three will become the first people to die at my touch. I have been fed enough now,"

Charleston had no idea what she meant but as black toxic smoke formed around the three of them, he knew this was nothing good.

"Why do this?" Augusta asked.

Charleston really hoped she was buying time or something. He looked but he didn't see his elven dagger. The Angel must have knocked it out of his hand during the fight.

The Angel laughed at Augusta.

He spotted the dagger a few metres away. He could always run and grab it but he would have to be extremely quick.

"You are a fool," The Angel said. "It doesn't matter why I do anything. I want to kill because I can do it and once I have the life force of everything on this planet then I will open a portal to the Realm of The Gods and I will devour them all,"

Augusta nodded and Charleston prepared himself to run.

"Now prepare to die," The Angel said.

Charleston charged forward.

The Angel roared.

Black deadly smoke wrapped around Augusta.

He grabbed the dagger.

Throwing it at the dragon.

The dagger slammed into Cargo's wing joint.

The Angel screamed.

Collapsing to the ground.

Augusta dashed forward.

Smashing the piece of orange cloth into Cargo's head.

The Angel screamed in agony as she was forced

out of her host.

CHAPTER 18

Augusta felt so damn happy as she forced the wonderful piece of orange cloth against Cargo's head and the air crackled, popped and banged as magical energy was unleashed.

The Angel screamed bloody murder so Augusta kept pressing the piece of cloth harder and harder against the Angel's foul head and she so badly wanted her best friend to return to her.

Within moments the orange cloth melted into Cargo and the Angel's scream changed but instead of pain it turned into one of agony and defeat.

Augusta backed away slowly as Cargo's possessed body curled, twisted and punched itself. The Angel was trying to kill Cargo but it wasn't working.

With a final scream and roar of friendly fire, Cargo spat out the Angel and a woman in black robes, a horrible thin veil and even now Augusta could tell that the woman's face was still made from dust and ash and dirt.

The Angel just knelt on the ground and Augusta could have sworn she was crying but she didn't care. The Angel had cost the lives of so many amazing people, like the brave elves, the strangely wonderful dwarves and the sensational crew of her flagship.

The Angel had lost this war.

Augusta went over to her and Charleston whipped out his swords and joined her.

"Do you not have anything to say for yourself?" Augusta asked.

The Angel laughed and coughed as large clumps of dust came out of her mouth and then Augusta understood that the stories were wrong. This was no ancient goddess from the elves, sure this spirit or Angel was deadly but she recognised this magic all too well.

The Angel was afflicted with the same dust magic that had meant the Jasper Raiders needed to wrap themselves up in orange wrappings. That was why the Angel wore a veil, wore long black robes and black boots.

She needed to keep herself together.

If the Angel could grin Augusta guessed she would be doing it now judging by how the Angel was staring at her.

"You finally figured out this was a trap to kill you, the elves and dwarves," The Angel said. "It wasn't meant to happen like this, you were all meant to die and your kingdoms were meant to fall so much easier,"

Augusta took out her sword and pierced the Angel's veil. Small amounts of dust and ash and dirt started to drip out.

"Is my kingdom under attack?" Augusta asked.

The Angel nodded and that only made more and more dust fall out. "That was the plan. Get you here and away from your kingdom whilst Jasper invaded in small groups,"

Augusta had to admit that Jasper was clever but she had had enough of her enemies being clever, and right now Augusta felt like she had a single advantage over the Emperor of Jasper.

She had Owen in charge of the Kingdom and she knew he was the second best person in the entire human lands to run the kingdom in her name. He was clever, brilliant and he always capitalised on how every single person thought he was dumb because he was gay.

Augusta was actually rather scared sometimes about what would happen if Owen turned on her, he was that clever that if Owen was really determined he could easily claim the kingdom for himself.

Thankfully Augusta knew that he wouldn't do that and he would buy her more than enough time to make sure she returned.

"Your life is forfeit," Augusta said.

Augusta thrusted the sword into the Angel's robes and watched as dust poured out of the wound instead of blood.

She heard Charleston come up behind her.

"Jasper is attacking our kingdom and they have magic I have never seen before. We need aid immediately,"

Augusta slowly nodded because they were in for a hell of a storm when they returned in a few days time but she still had faith in her rising power, her people and the man she loved. They would find a way but first Augusta wanted to see if her best friend in the entire world was okay.

It was the least she could do because Cargo was a lot more than a mere dragon, he was a fighter, a transport method and most importantly he was her best friend in the entire world.

And she always protected her friends no matter how dire the odds seemed.

CHAPTER 19

A few hours later after everyone had all joined in together to do a final sweep of the islands and make sure there were no more Jasper tricks around, Charleston, Augusta and Glumpy stood on a white sandy beach at the very edge of the ring of islands.

Charleston watched Cargo flapping about and it was so great, wonderful and relaxing to see him so happy again. He hated to imagine what it must have been like in that tiny piece of orange cloth, let alone be stuck under Augusta's sweaty feet for so long.

That must have been torture for the poor dragon.

But as much as Charleston was surprised about it, he was actually going to miss these islands. They were so beautiful and even the one they were standing on with its oval shape, white sand and ten palm trees that blew slightly in the warm breeze just felt magical.

The air was calm and warm and had hints of sea salt in it and Charleston knew he was going to miss it but maybe he could return one day, hopefully under less bloody conditions.

Because that was the thing about all of this, they were all just chess pieces in the eternal game between different leaders, countries and powers. Charleston really wanted Augusta to win against Jasper but Jasper was clearly a hell of a lot smarter than he had ever thought possible.

The Emperor of Jasper had a lot of time on his hands if he had managed to create such a complex trap that had basically killed any forces had could possibly hope to challenge him.

"Well lassie and laddie, this is our goodbyes then. Ah, I have enjoyed our time together and I just look forward to drowning in ale even more!" Glumpy shouted.

Charleston couldn't believe he was actually going to miss the dwarf too. Damn this trip had changed him.

"And our deal still stands?" Augusta asked.

"Of course las. Our dwarfs ain't gonna let any Jasper scum touch our weapons, supplies or ale. We gonna our ale and drink it ourselves,"

Charleston laughed. Dwarves really were something special.

Glumpy took a step closer. "I already sent me word to the King about sending troops to your kingdom sooner. They should be there by the time your dragon flies ya back,"

"Thank you," Augusta said. "I hope we meet

again,"

"Ah, me too las. Come down the pub whenever you like and I drink ya under the table any day,"

As the little dwarf hopped (or ran) across the white sandy beach towards his speedboat, Charleston just felt hopeful about the future because the dwarves would come to their aid, and he had actually seen first hand that only idiots messed with dwarves and their ale.

"We have to start flying soon," Augusta said. "I want a kingdom to get back to and I know the elves are angry about the King's death,"

"What did they say?" Charleston asked, knowing Augusta had had a quick conversation with one about an hour ago.

"The elves will make it to Octogi to help us but they are angry. They are livid with Jasper and they want to send every single elf in their Empire to our shores,"

Charleston could only nod. That would have to be thousands, if not millions of elves on their shores. It would be amazing but the idea of having to coordinate with that many people would just be a nightmare.

"Whatever happened to those creatures the Jasper Raiders had?" Charleston asked.

Augusta's laughter was so beautiful as she pointed towards stunning black-skinned snakes the size of warships swimming peacefully about in the water.

"They were never evil creatures in the first place. I believe whoever created the black stone prisons to store that they was abusing them into service. Now they are free to do whatever they want with their Jasper masters dead,"

That really was great news.

Charleston was about to ask about the Jasper navy that was meant to be coming but on the horizon he saw ten black flags of Jasper warships but he also saw tons of elven ships glide and dance and swirl elegantly through the water.

Within moments the Jasper fleet was destroyed and Charleston felt amazing about that. At least their enemy was weakened even more.

Cargo flew back gently and landed in the water and Charleston hugged the beautiful dragon who's bright blue scales shone in the late afternoon sun.

"We have a lot to do and not a lot of time to do it in," Augusta said.

Charleston helped the love of his life onboard her best friend and then he joined her, and as Cargo started the three day journey of flying away from the ring islands back towards home, Charleston felt at peace and finally like Augusta's kingdom was a rising force capable of destroying Jasper once and for all.

Jasper was cut off from elven and dwarf trade, they had lost the Jasper Raiders and the Angel of Death and most importantly him and Augusta had survived.

Sure they might be being invaded but that was a

problem for three's days time. For now he was going to enjoy the journey, love his wonderful girlfriend and prepare himself for the battle ahead.

Because it would certainly be a battle to end all battles and the fate of humanity rested on them not failing.

GET YOUR FREE AND EXCLUSIVE SHORT STORY NOW! LEARN ABOUT NEMESIO'S PAST!

https://www.subscribepage.com/fireheart

About the author:

Connor Whiteley is the author of over 60 books in the sci-fi fantasy, nonfiction psychology and books for writer's genre and he is a Human Branding Speaker and Consultant.

He is a passionate warhammer 40,000 reader, psychology student and author.

Who narrates his own audiobooks and he hosts The Psychology World Podcast.

All whilst studying Psychology at the University of Kent, England.

Also, he was a former Explorer Scout where he gave a speech to the Maltese President in August 2018 and he attended Prince Charles' 70th Birthday Party at Buckingham Palace in May 2018.

Plus, he is a self-confessed coffee lover!

Other books by Connor Whiteley:

Bettie English Private Eye Series
A Very Private Woman
The Russian Case
A Very Urgent Matter
A Case Most Personal
Trains, Scots and Private Eyes
The Federation Protects

Lord of War Origin Trilogy:
Not Scared Of The Dark
Madness
Burn Them All

The Fireheart Fantasy Series
Heart of Fire
Heart of Lies
Heart of Prophecy
Heart of Bones
Heart of Fate

City of Assassins (Urban Fantasy)
City of Death
City of Marytrs
City of Pleasure
City of Power

Agents of The Emperor
Return of The Ancient Ones
Vigilance
Angels of Fire
Kingmaker
The Eight
The Lost Generation
Hunt
Emperor's Council
Speaker of Treachery
Birth Of The Empire
Terraforma

The Rising Augusta Fantasy Adventure Series
Rise To Power
Rising Walls
Rising Force
Rising Realm

Lord Of War Trilogy (Agents of The Emperor)
Not Scared Of The Dark
Madness
Burn It All Down

Gay Romance Novellas
Breaking, Nursing, Repairing A Broken Heart
Jacob And Daniel
Fallen For A Lie
Spying And Weddings

The Garro Series- Fantasy/Sci-fi
GARRO: GALAXY'S END
GARRO: RISE OF THE ORDER
GARRO: END TIMES
GARRO: SHORT STORIES
GARRO: COLLECTION
GARRO: HERESY
GARRO: FAITHLESS
GARRO: DESTROYER OF WORLDS
GARRO: COLLECTIONS BOOK 4-6
GARRO: MISTRESS OF BLOOD
GARRO: BEACON OF HOPE
GARRO: END OF DAYS

Winter Series- Fantasy Trilogy Books
WINTER'S COMING
WINTER'S HUNT
WINTER'S REVENGE
WINTER'S DISSENSION

Miscellaneous:
RETURN
FREEDOM
SALVATION
Reflection of Mount Flame
The Masked One
The Great Deer
English Independence

OTHER SHORT STORIES BY CONNOR WHITELEY

Mystery Short Story Collections
Criminally Good Stories Volume 1: 20 Detective Mystery Short Stories
Criminally Good Stories Volume 2: 20 Private Investigator Short Stories
Criminally Good Stories Volume 3: 20 Crime Fiction Short Stories
Criminally Good Stories Volume 4: 20 Science Fiction and Fantasy Mystery Short Stories
Criminally Good Stories Volume 5: 20 Romantic Suspense Short Stories

Mystery Short Stories:
Protecting The Woman She Hated
Finding A Royal Friend

Our Woman In Paris
Corrupt Driving
A Prime Assassination
Jubilee Thief
Jubilee, Terror, Celebrations
Negative Jubilation
Ghostly Jubilation
Killing For Womenkind
A Snowy Death
Miracle Of Death
A Spy In Rome
The 12:30 To St Pancreas
A Country In Trouble
A Smokey Way To Go
A Spicy Way To GO
A Marketing Way To Go
A Missing Way To Go
A Showering Way To Go
Poison In The Candy Cane
Christmas Innocence
You Better Watch Out
Christmas Theft
Trouble In Christmas
Smell of The Lake
Problem In A Car
Theft, Past and Team
Embezzler In The Room

A Strange Way To Go
A Horrible Way To Go
Ann Awful Way To Go
An Old Way To Go
A Fishy Way To Go
A Pointy Way To Go
A High Way To Go
A Fiery Way To Go
A Glassy Way To Go
A Chocolatey Way To Go
Kendra Detective Mystery Collection Volume 1
Kendra Detective Mystery Collection Volume 2
Stealing A Chance At Freedom
Glassblowing and Death
Theft of Independence
Cookie Thief
Marble Thief
Book Thief
Art Thief
Mated At The Morgue
The Big Five Whoopee Moments
Stealing An Election
Mystery Short Story Collection Volume 1
Mystery Short Story Collection Volume 2
Criminal Performance

Candy Detectives
Key To Birth In The Past

<u>Science Fiction Short Stories:</u>
Temptation
Superhuman Autospy
Blood In The Redwater
All Is Dust
Vigil
Emperor Forgive Us
Their Brave New World
Gummy Bear Detective
The Candy Detective
What Candies Fear
The Blurred Image
Shattered Legions
The First Rememberer
Life of A Rememberer
System of Wonder
Lifesaver
Remarkable Way She Died
The Interrogation of Annabella Stormic
Blade of The Emperor
Arbiter's Truth
Computation of Battle
Old One's Wrath
Puppets and Masters

Ship of Plague
Interrogation
Edge of Failure
One Way Choice
Acceptable Losses
Balance of Power
Good Idea At The Time
Escape Plan
Escape In The Hesitation
Inspiration In Need
Singing Warriors
Knowledge is Power
Killer of Polluters
Climate of Death
The Family Mailing Affair
Defining Criminality
The Martian Affair
A Cheating Affair
The Little Café Affair
Mountain of Death
Prisoner's Fight
Claws of Death
Bitter Air
Honey Hunt
Blade On A Train
<u>Fantasy Short Stories:</u>
City of Snow

City of Light
City of Vengeance
Dragons, Goats and Kingdom
Smog The Pathetic Dragon
Don't Go In The Shed
The Tomato Saver
The Remarkable Way She Died
The Bloodied Rose
Asmodia's Wrath
Heart of A Killer
Emissary of Blood
Dragon Coins
Dragon Tea
Dragon Rider
Sacrifice of the Soul
Heart of The Flesheater
Heart of The Regent
Heart of The Standing
Feline of The Lost
Heart of The Story
City of Fire
Awaiting Death

All books in 'An Introductory Series':
Careers In Psychology
Psychology of Suicide
Dementia Psychology
Clinical Psychology Reflections Volume 4
Forensic Psychology of Terrorism And Hostage-Taking
Forensic Psychology of False Allegations
Year In Psychology
CBT For Anxiety
CBT For Depression
Applied Psychology
BIOLOGICAL PSYCHOLOGY 3RD EDITION
COGNITIVE PSYCHOLOGY THIRD EDITION
SOCIAL PSYCHOLOGY- 3RD EDITION
ABNORMAL PSYCHOLOGY 3RD EDITION
PSYCHOLOGY OF RELATIONSHIPS- 3RD EDITION
DEVELOPMENTAL PSYCHOLOGY 3RD EDITION
HEALTH PSYCHOLOGY
RESEARCH IN PSYCHOLOGY
A GUIDE TO MENTAL HEALTH AND TREATMENT AROUND THE WORLD-

A GLOBAL LOOK AT DEPRESSION
FORENSIC PSYCHOLOGY
THE FORENSIC PSYCHOLOGY OF THEFT, BURGLARY AND OTHER CRIMES AGAINST PROPERTY
CRIMINAL PROFILING: A FORENSIC PSYCHOLOGY GUIDE TO FBI PROFILING AND GEOGRAPHICAL AND STATISTICAL PROFILING.
CLINICAL PSYCHOLOGY
FORMULATION IN PSYCHOTHERAPY
PERSONALITY PSYCHOLOGY AND INDIVIDUAL DIFFERENCES
CLINICAL PSYCHOLOGY REFLECTIONS VOLUME 1
CLINICAL PSYCHOLOGY REFLECTIONS VOLUME 2
Clinical Psychology Reflections Volume 3
CULT PSYCHOLOGY
Police Psychology

A Psychology Student's Guide To University
How Does University Work?
A Student's Guide To University And Learning
University Mental Health and Mindset

www.ingramcontent.com/pod-product-compliance
Lightning Source LLC
LaVergne TN
LVHW012120070526
838202LV00056B/5801